Kiki's Magic Afro

CW00860397

By Miriam Gay

Copyright © 2018 Miriam Gay
All rights reserved.

ISBN-13: 978-1718689312

DEDICATION

For my darling Daughter Kamiah .xx

Kiki's Magic Afro

Magical Adventure:
Book 1

Kiki's afro was beautiful and wild
Magnificent and vibrant for such a young
child.
There were so many things Kiki could do
with her hair
but for most of the time she preferred it just
there.

The kids at school would laugh and make fun
"Your hair looks crazy, what have you done!"
Kiki would cry and feel really sad
"But I love my hair, is it really that bad?"

"Everyone in my family has hair like this, my mum, my dad and my big sister Liz.
But maybe they're right, it mustn't be that great.
I'm going to do something about it straight away!"

When Kiki arrived home she went straight upstairs and stared in the mirror with a look of despair.
"Oh Afro if you're all that great, do something right now"...suddenly her hair began to shake.

Kiki jumped back, "Did my hair just move? It usually stands still just like the big moon". She crept back to the mirror to take another look and once again her afro shook.

Bright crazy colours began to flash around her head.
Yellow, pink, blue, green and red.

The coils of her hair started to bounce and twist.
Kiki ran out the room to find her big sister Liz.

"Liz Liz Liz! My afro is alive, it moved and twisted and there's bright colours inside!" "Don't be silly", her sister Liz laughed. "Your hair can't move", as she tugged her plaits.

"Well maybe yours doesn't because your hair is cornrowed".
"Well mine must be magic...it's my magic Afro!"

"I can't wait to show everyone at school,
they'll see my hair and think I'm cool"
"Embrace your natural hair Kiki", said her
afro out loud
"Oh I love my hair all big and wild!"
"It's fun, magic and part of me
Oh magic afro I love you indeed!"

The End

Printed in Great Britain
by Amazon

43224789R10015